The Vortex Blaster

E. E. Smith

Alpha Editions

This edition published in 2024

ISBN : 9789364731966

Design and Setting By
Alpha Editions
www.alphaedis.com
Email - info@alphaedis.com

As per information held with us this book is in Public Domain.
This book is a reproduction of an important historical work. Alpha Editions uses the best technology to reproduce historical work in the same manner it was first published to preserve its original nature. Any marks or number seen are left intentionally to preserve its true form.

Contents

CHAPTER ONE ....- 1 -
CHAPTER TWO ....- 4 -
CHAPTER THREE ....- 9 -
CHAPTER FOUR..- 17 -

CHAPTER ONE

Storm Cloud—the Vortex Blaster!

Doctor Neal Cloud had once been a normal human being, gregarious and neighborly. He had been concerned as little with death as is the normal human being. Death was an abstraction. It was inevitable, of course, but it could not actually touch him or affect him personally, except at some unspecified, unconsidered and remote future time.

For twenty uneventful years he worked in the Atomic Research Laboratory of the Galactic Patrol, seeking a way to extinguish the "loose" atomic vortices resulting from the breaking out of control of atomic power plants. At home he had had wife Jo and their three kids—and what Jo had meant to him can be described adequately only in mathematical, not emotional terms. They had formed practically a closed system.

Hence, when a loose atomic vortex crashed to earth through his home, destroying in an instant everything that had made life worthwhile—Doctor Cloud had changed.

He had had something to live for; he had loved life. Then—suddenly—he had not, and he did not.

Cloud had always been a mathematical prodigy. Given the various activity values of a vortex at any instant, he knew exactly the "sigma" (summation) curve. Or, given the curve itself, he knew every individual reading of which it was composed—all without knowing how he did it. Nevertheless, he had never tried to blow out a vortex with duodec. He wanted to live, and it was a mathematical certainty that that very love of life would so impede his perceptions that he would die in the attempt.

Then came disaster. While still numb with the shock of it, he decided to blow out the oldest and worst vortex on Earth; partly in revenge, partly in the cold hope that he would fail and die, as so many hundreds of good men had already died.

But it was the vortex that died, not Cloud. It was a near thing, but when he was released from the hospital he found himself the most famous man alive. He was "Storm" Cloud, the Vortex Blaster—Civilization's only vortex blaster!

He had now extinguished hundreds of the things. The operation, once so thrilling to others, had become a drab routine to him.

But he had not recovered and never would recover a normal outlook upon life. Something within him had died with his Jo, a vital something had been torn from the innermost depths of his being. That terrible psychic wound was no longer stamped boldly upon him for all to see—it no longer made it impossible for him to work with other men or for other men to work with him—but it was there.

Thus he preferred to be alone. Whenever he decently could, he traveled alone, and worked alone.

He was alone now, hurtling through a barren region of space toward Rift Seventy-one and the vortex which was next upon his list. In the interests of time-saving and safety—minions of the Drug Syndicate had taken him by force from a passenger liner not long since, in order to save from extinction a vortex which they were using in their nefarious business—he was driving a light cruiser converted to one-man control. In one special hold lay his vortex-blasting flitter; in others were his vast assortment of duodec bombs and other stores and supplies.

And as he drove along through those strangely barren, unsurveyed wastes, he thought, as always, of Jo. He had not as yet actually courted death. He had not considered such courting necessary. Everyone had supposed, and he himself hoped, that a vortex would get him in spite of everything he could do. That hope was gone—it was as simple to blow out a vortex as a match.

But it would be *so* easy to make a slip—and a tiny little bit of a slip would be enough.... No, the Vortex Blaster simply couldn't put such a black mark as that on his record. But if something else came along he might lean just a trifle toward it....

A distress call came in, pitifully, woefully weak—the distress call of a warm-blooded oxygen-breather!

It would have to be weak, upon his low-powered apparatus, Cloud reflected, as he sprang to attention and began to manipulate his controls. He was a good eighty-five parsecs—at least an hour at maximum blast—from the nearest charted traffic route.

He could not possibly get there in time. When anything happened in space it usually happened fast—it was almost always a question of seconds, not of hours. Cloud worked fast, but even so he had no time even to acknowledge—he was just barely in time to catch upon his communicator-plate a tiny but brilliant flash of light as the frantic sending ceased.

Whatever had occurred was already history.

Nevertheless, he had to investigate. He had received the call and it was possible, even probable, that no other spaceship had been within range. Law and tradition were alike adamant that every such call must be heeded by any vessel receiving it, of whatever class or upon whatever mission bound. He hurled out a call of his own, with all of his small power. No reply—the ether was empty.

Driving toward the scene of catastrophe at max, Cloud did what little he could do. He had never witnessed a space emergency before, but he knew the routine.

There was no use whatever in investigating the wreck itself. The brilliance of the flare had been evidence enough to the physicist that that vessel and everything too near it had ceased to exist. It was lifeboats he was after. They were supposed to stick around to be rescued, but out here they probably would not—they would head for the nearest planet to be sure of air. Air was far more important than either water or food—and lifeboats, by the very nature of things, could not carry enough air.

Approaching the charted spot, he sent out the universal "*survivors?*" call and swept all nearby space with his detectors—fruitlessly.

But this was not conclusive. Since his cruiser was intended solely to get him safely from one planet to another, he had only low-power, short-range detectors. Of course, his communicator, weak as it was, could reach two or three times as far as any lifeboat could possibly be—but he had heard more than once of lifeboats, jammed full of women and children, being launched into space without anyone aboard who could operate even a communicator. It required only a few minutes to pick out the nearest sun. As he shot toward it he kept his detectors fanning out ahead, combing space mile by plotted cubic mile. And when he was halfway to that sun his plate revealed a lifeboat. It was very close to the solar system toward which Cloud was blasting—entering it—nearing one of the planets. Guided by his plate, he drove home a solid communicator beam.

Still no answer!

Either the lifeboat did not have a communicator—some of the older types didn't—or else it was smashed, or nobody aboard could run it. He'd have to keep his plate on them and follow them down to the ground.

But what was that? Another boat on the plate? Not a lifeboat—too big, but not big enough to be a regular spaceship. It was coming out from the planet, apparently. To rescue? No—what the hell! The lug was beaming the lifeboat!

"Let's go, you sheet-iron lummox!" the Blaster cried aloud, kicking in his every remaining watt of drive. Then, eyes upon his plate, he swore viciously, corrosively.

CHAPTER TWO

The Boneheads of Dhil

The planet Dhil and its enormous satellite, called "Lune" in lieu of the utterly unpronounceable name its inhabitants gave it, are almost twin worlds, revolving about their common center of gravity and circling as one about their sun in its second orbit. In the third orbit revolves Uhal, a planet strikingly similar to Dhil in every respect of gravity, atmosphere, and climate. Furthermore, Dhilians and Uhalians are, to all interests and purposes, identical.[1]

In spite of these facts, however, the two peoples had been at war with each other, most of the time, for centuries. Practically all of this warfare had been waged upon luckless Lune.

Each race was well advanced in science, and each had atomic power, offensive beams, defensive screens. Neither had even partial inertialessness, neither had ever driven a spaceship to any other solar system, neither had ever heard of Galactic Civilization.

At this particular time peace of a sort existed. More precisely, it was a truce of exhaustion and preparation for further strife. It was a fragile thing indeed, and existed only upon the surface. Beneath, the conflict raged as bitterly as ever. The discovery by the scientists, inventors or secret service of either world of any superior artifice of destruction would kindle the conflagration anew, without warning.

Such was the condition obtaining when Darjeeb of Uhal blasted his little spaceship upward away from Lune. He was glowing with pride of accomplishment, suffused with self-esteem. Not only had he touched off an inextinguishable atomic flame exactly where it would do the most good, but as a crowning achievement he had taken and was now making off with no less a personage than Luda of Dhil herself—the coldest, hardest, most efficient Minister of War that the planet Dhil had ever had!

Now, as soon as they could extract certain facts from Luda's mind, they could take Lune in short order. Then, with Lune definitely theirs to use as a permanent base, Dhil could not possibly hold out for more than a couple of years or so. The goal of generations would have been reached—he, Darjeeb, would have wealth, fame and—best of all—power!

Gazing gloatingly at his furiously radiating captive with every eye he could bring to bear, Darjeeb strolled over to inspect again her chains and manacles. Let her radiate!

She could not touch his mind; no mentality in existence could break down his barriers.

But physically, she had to be watched. Those irons were strong, but so was Luda. If she could succeed in breaking free he would very probably have to shoot her, which would be a very bad thing indeed. She had not caved in yet, but she would. When he got her to Uhal, where the proper measures could be taken, she would give up every scrap of knowledge she had ever had!

The chains were holding, all eight of them, and Darjeeb kept on gloating as he backed toward his control station. To him Luda's shape was normal enough, since his own was the same, but in the sight of a Tellurian she would have appeared more than a little queer.

The lower part of her resembled more or less closely a small elephant, one weighing perhaps three hundred and fifty pounds. There were, however, differences. The skin was clear and fine, delicately tanned; there were no ears or tusks; the neck was longer. The trunk was shorter, divided at the tip to form a highly capable hand; and between the somewhat protuberant eyes of this "feeding" head there thrust out a boldly Roman, startlingly human nose. The brain in this head was very small, being concerned only in the matter of food.

Above this not-too-unbelievable body, however, all resemblance to anything Terrestrial ceased. Instead of a back there were two mighty shoulders, fore and aft, from each of which sprang two tremendous arms, like the trunk except longer and stronger. Between those massive shoulders there was an armored, slightly retractile neck which carried the heavily armored "thinking" head. In this head there were no mouths, no nostrils. The four equally-spaced pairs of eyes were protected and shielded by heavy ridges and plates. The entire head, except for its juncture with the neck, was solidly sheathed with bare, hard, thick, tough bone.

Darjeeb's amazing head shone a clean-scrubbed white. But Luda's—the eternal feminine!—was really something to look at. It had been sanded, buffed, and polished. It had been inlaid with bars and strips and scrolls of variously colored noble metals and alloys; then decorated tastefully in red and green and blue and black enamel—then, to cap the climax, *lacquered*!

But that was old stuff to Darjeeb. All that he cared about was the tightness of the chains immobilizing Luda's every hand and foot. Seeing that they were all tight, he returned his attention to his plates. For he was not yet in the clear. Any number of enemies might be blasting off after him at any minute....

A light flashed upon his panel—something was in the ether. Behind him everything was clear. Nothing was coming from Dhil. Ah, there it was—coming in from open space. Nothing *could* move that fast, but this thing, whatever it might be, certainly was. It was a space-craft of some kind. And, gods of the ancients, *how* it was coming!

As a matter of fact the lifeboat was coming in at less than one light, the merest crawl, as space-speeds go. Otherwise Darjeeb could not have seen it at all. Even that velocity, however, was so utterly beyond anything known to his solar system that the usually phlegmatic Uhalian sat spellbound—appalled—for a fraction of a second. Then every organ leaping convulsively in the realization that that incredible thing was actually happening, he drove one hand toward a control.

Too late—before the hand had covered half the distance, the incomprehensibly fast ship had struck his own in direct central impact. In fact, before he even realized what was happening it was all over! The strange vessel had struck and had stopped dead-still—without a jar or shock, without even a vibration!

Both ships should have been blasted to atoms—but there the stranger was, poised motionless beside him. Then, under the urge of a ridiculously tiny jet of flame, she leaped away, covering a distance of miles in the twinkling of an eye. Then something else happened. She moved aside, drifting heavily backward *against* the stupendous force of her full driving blast!

As soon as he recovered from his shock, Darjeeb's cold, keen brain began to function in its wonted fashion.

Only one explanation was possible—*inertialessness*!

What a weapon! With that and Luda—even without Luda—the solar system was his. No longer was it a question of Uhal overcoming Dhil. With inertialessness, he himself would become the dictator, not only of Uhal and Dhil and Lune, but also of all the worlds within reach.

That vessel and its secrets *must* be his!

He blasted, then, to match the inert velocity of the smaller craft. As his ship crept toward the other he reached out both telepathically—he could neither speak nor hear—and with a spy-ray, to determine the most feasible method of taking over this godsend.

Bipeds! Peculiar little beasts—repulsive. Only two arms and two eyes—only one head. Weak, soft, fragile, but they might have weapons. No, no weapons—good! Couldn't *any* of them communicate? Ah yes, there was one—an unusually thin, reed-like specimen, bundled up in layer after layer of fabric....

I perceive that you are the survivors of some catastrophe in outer space. Tell your pilot to open up, so that I may come aboard and guide you to safety, Darjeeb began. He correlated instantly, if unsympathetically, the smashed panel and the pilot's bleeding head. If the creature had had a real head it could have wrecked a dozen such things with it without getting a scratch. *Hurry! Those may come at any moment who will destroy all of us without palaver.*

I am trying, sir, but I cannot get through to him direct. It will take a few moments, the strange telepathist replied. She began to wave rhythmically her peculiar arms, hands, and fingers. Others of the outlanders brandished their members and made repulsive motions with their ridiculous mouths. Finally—

He says that he would rather not, the interpreter reported. *He asks you to go ahead. He will follow you down.*

Impossible—we cannot land upon this world or upon its primary, Dhil, Darjeeb argued, reasonably. *These people are enemies—savages—I have just escaped from them. It is death to attempt to land anywhere in this system except upon my home planet Uhal—that bluish one.*

Very well, then, we'll see you over there. We are just about out of air, but it will take only a minute or so to reach Uhal.

But that would not do either, of course. Argument took too much time. He would have to use force, and he had better call up reenforcements. Darjeeb hurled mental orders to a henchman far below, threw out his magnetic grapples, and turned on a broad, low-powered beam.

Open up or die! he ordered. *I do not want to blast you open—but time presses, and I will do so if I must!*

That treatment was effective, as the Uhalian had been pretty certain that it would be. Pure heat is hard to take. The outer portal opened and Darjeeb, after donning his armor and checking his ray-gun, picked Luda up and swung nonchalantly out into space. Luda was tough enough so that a little vacuum wouldn't hurt her—much. Inside the lifeboat he tossed his trussed-up captive into an unoccupied corner and strode purposefully toward the control board.

I want to know—right now—what it is that makes this ship to be without inertia, he radiated harshly.

The Chickladorian at the board—the only male aboard the lifeboat—was very plainly in bad shape. He had been fighting off unconsciousness for hours. The beaming had not done him a bit of good. Nevertheless he paid no attention to the invading monstrosity's relayed demand, but concentrated what was left of his intelligence upon his visibeam communicator.

"You'll have to hurry it up," he said quietly, in "spaceal", the lingua franca of deep space. "The ape's aboard and means business. I'm blacking out, I'm afraid, but I've left the lock open for you. Take over, pal!"

Darjeeb had been probing vainly at the pink biped's mind. Most peculiar—a natural mind-block of tremendous power!

Tell him to give me what I want to know or I will squeeze it out of his very brain, he directed the Manarkan girl.

As the order was being translated he slipped an arm out of his suit and clamped one huge hand around the pilot's head. But just as he made contact, before he had applied any pressure at all, the weakling fainted—went limp and useless.

Simultaneously, he saw in the visiplate that another ship, neither Uhalian nor Dhilian, had arrived and had locked on.

He tautened as two of his senses registered disquieting tidings. He received, as plainly as though it were intended for him, a welcome which the swaddled-up biped was radiating in delight at an unexpected visitor. He saw that that visitor, now entering the compartment, while a biped, was in no sense on a par with the frightened, helpless, wholly innocuous creatures already cluttering up the room. Instead, it was armed and armored—in complete readiness for strife even with Darjeeb of Uhal!

The Bonehead swung his ready weapon—with his build, he had no need, ever, to turn or whirl to face danger—and pressed a stud. A searing lance of flame stabbed out at the over-bold intruder. Passengers screamed and fled into whatever places of safety were available.

CHAPTER THREE

DeLameters and Space-Axe!

Cloud wasted no time in swearing; he could swear and act simultaneously. He flashed his cruiser up near the lifeboat, went inert, and began to match velocities even before the Uhalian's heat-beam expired. Since his intrinsic was not very far off, as such things go, it wouldn't take him very long, and he'd need all the time to get ready for what he had to do. He conferred briefly with the boat's Chickladorian pilot upon his visual, then thought intensely.

He would have to board the lifeboat—he didn't see any other way out of it. Even if he had anything to blast it with, he couldn't without killing innocent people. And he didn't have much offensive stuff; his cruiser was not a warship. She carried plenty of defense, but no heavy offensive beams at all.

He had two suits of armor, a G-P regulation and his vortex special, which was even stronger. He had his DeLameters. He had four semi-portables and two needle-beams, for excavating. He had thousands of duodec bombs, not one of which could be detonated by anything less violent than the furious heart of a loose atomic vortex.

What else? Nothing—or yes, there was his sampler. He grinned as he looked at it. About the size of a tack-hammer, with a needle point on one side and a razor blade on the other. It had a handle three feet long. A deceptive little thing, truly, for it weighed fifteen pounds and that tiny blade could shear through neocarballoy as cleanly as a steel knife slices through cheese. It was made of dureum, that peculiar synthetic which, designed primarily for use in hyper-spatial tubes, had become of wide utility. Considering what terrific damage a Valerian could do with a space-axe, he should be able to do quite a bit with this. It ought to qualify at least as a space-hatchet!

He put on his special armor, set his DeLameters to maximum intensity at minimum aperture, and hung the hatchet upon a hook at his belt. He eased off his blasts—there, the velocities matched. A minute's work with needle-beam, tractors and pressors sufficed to cut the two smaller ships apart and to dispose of the Uhalian's magnets and cables. Another minute of careful manipulation and the cruiser had taken the Uhalian's place. He swung out, locked the cruiser's outer portal behind him, and entered the lifeboat.

As Cloud stepped into the boat's saloon he was met by a lethal, high-intensity beam. He had not really expected such an instantaneous, undeclared war, but he was ready for it.

Every screen he had was full out, his left hand held poised and ready at his hip on a screened DeLameter. His return blast was practically a reflection of

Darjeeb's bolt, and it did vastly more damage, for the Uhalian had made an error!

The hand which held the ray-gun was the one which had been manhandling the pilot, and the monster had not had time, quite, to get it back inside his screens. In the fury of Cloud's riposte, gun and hand disappeared, as did a square foot of panel behind them. But Darjeeb had other hands and other guns, and for seconds blinding rays raved out against unyielding defensive screens.

Neither screen went down. The Tellurian holstered his DeLameter. It would not take much of this stuff, he reflected, to kill some of the passengers remaining in the saloon. He'd go in with his hatchet!

He lugged it up and leaped, driving straight forward at the flaming projectors, with all of his mass and strength going into the swing of his weapon. The enemy did not dodge, merely threw up a hand to flick aside with his gun-barrel the descending toy.

Cloud grinned fleetingly as he realized what the other must be thinking—that the man must be puny indeed to be making such ado in wielding such a tiny, trifling thing. For, to anyone not familiar with dureum, it is sheerly unbelievable that so much mass and momentum can possibly reside in so small a bulk.

Thus, when fiercely-driven cutting edge met opposing ray-gun, it did not waver or deflect. It scarcely even slowed. Through the metal of the gun that vicious blade sliced resistlessly, shearing off fingers as it sped. And on down, urged by everything Cloud's powerful frame could deliver. Through armor it punched, through the bony plating covering that tremendous double shoulder, deep into the flesh and bone of the shoulder itself. So deep that its penetration was stopped only by the impact of the hatchet's haft against the armor.

Under the impetus of the man's furious attack both battlers went down. The unwounded Tellurian, however, was the first to recover control. Cloud's mailed hands were still clamped to the sampler's grips, and, using his weapon as a staff, he scrambled to his feet. He planted one steel boot upon the helmet's dome, got a momentary stance with the other thrust into the angle between barrel body and flailing leg, bent his burly back and heaved. The deeply-embedded blade tore out through bone and flesh and metal—and as it did so the two rear cabled arms dropped limp, useless!

That mighty rear shoulder and its appurtenances were thoroughly *hors du combat*. The monster still had one good hand, however—and he was still in the fight!

That hand flashed out, to seize the hatchet and to wield it against its owner. It was fast, too—but not quite fast enough. The man, strongly braced, yanked backward, the weapon's needle point and keen blade tearing through flesh and snicking off clutching fingers as it was hauled away. Then Cloud swung his axe aloft and poised, making it abundantly clear that the next stroke would be straight down into the top of the Uhalian's head.

That was enough. The monster backed away, every eye aglare, and Cloud stepped warily over to the captive, Luda. A couple of strokes of his trenchant sampler gave him a length of chain. Then, working carefully to keep his wounded foe threatened at every instant, he worked the chain into a tight loop around Darjeeb's neck, pulled it unmercifully taut around a stanchion, and welded it there with his DeLameter.

Nor did he trust the other monster unreservedly, bound though she was. In fact, he did not trust her at all. In spite of family rows, like has a tendency to fight with like against a common foe! But since she was not wearing armor, she didn't stand a chance against a DeLameter. Hence, he could now take time to look around the saloon.

The pilot, lying flat upon the floor, was beginning to come to. Not quite flat, either, for a shapely Chickladorian girl, wearing the forty-one square inches of covering which was *de rigeur* in her eyes, had his head cushioned upon one bare leg, and was sobbing gibberish over him. That wouldn't help. Cloud started toward the first-aid cabinet, but stopped. A white-wrapped figure was already bending over the injured man, administering something out of a black bottle. He knew what it was—kedeselin. That was what he had been going after himself, but he would not have dared to give even a hippopotamus such a terrific jolt as she was pouring into him. She must be a nurse and a top-ranker—but Cloud shivered in sympathy.

The pilot stiffened convulsively, then relaxed. His eyes rolled; he gasped and shuddered; but he came to life and sat up groggily.

"What goes on here?" Cloud demanded ungently, in spaceal. The Chickladorian's wounds had already been bandaged. Nothing more could be done for him until they could get him to a hospital, and he *had* to report before he blacked out entirely.

"I don't know," the pink man made answer, recovering by the minute. "All the ape said, as near as I could get it, was that I had to show him all about inertialessness."

He then spoke rapidly to the girl—his wife, Cloud guessed—who was still holding him fervently.

The pink girl nodded. Then, catching Cloud's eye, she pointed at the two monstrosities, then at the Manarkan nurse standing calmly near by. Startlingly slim, swathed to the eyes in billows of glamorette, she looked as fragile as a reed—but Cloud knew that appearances were highly deceptive in that case. She, too, nodded at the Tellurian, then talked rapidly in sign language to a short, thick-muscled woman of some race entirely strange to the Blaster. She was used to going naked; that was very evident. She had been wearing a light robe of convention, but it had been pretty well demolished in the melee and she did not realize that what was left of it was hanging in tatters down her broad back. The "squatty" eyed the gesticulating Manarkan and spoke in a beautifully modulated, deep bass voice to the Chickladorian eyeful, who in turn passed the message along to her husband.

"The bonehead you had the argument with says to hell with you," the pilot translated finally into spaceal. "Says his mob will be out here after him directly, and if you don't cut him loose and give him all the dope on our Bergs he'll give us all the beam—plenty."

Luda was, meanwhile, trying to attract attention. She was bouncing up and down, rattling her chains, rolling her eyes, and in general demanding notice of all.

More communication ensued, culminating in, "The one with the fancy-worked skull—she's a frail, but not the other bonehead's frail, I guess—says pay no attention to the ape. He's a murderer, a pirate, a bum, a louse, and so forth, she says. Says to take your axe and cut his damn head clean off, chuck his carcass out the port, and get to hell out of here as fast as you can blast."

Cloud figured that that might be sound advice, at that, but he didn't want to take such drastic steps without more comprehensive data.

"Why?" he asked.

But this was too much for the communications relays to handle. Cloud realized that he did not know spaceal at all well, since he had not been out in deep space very long. He knew that spaceal was a simple language, not well adapted to the accurate expression of subtle nuances of meaning. And all those intermediate translations were garbling things terrifically. He was not surprised that nothing much was coming through, even though the prettied-up monster was by this time practically throwing a fit.

"She's quit trying to spin her yarn," the Chickladorian said finally. "She says she's been trying to talk to you direct, but she can't get through. Says to unseal your ports—cut your screens—let down your barrier—something like that. Don't know what she does mean, exactly. None of us does except maybe the Manarkan, and she can't get it across on her fingers."

"Oh, my thought-screen!" Cloud exclaimed, and cut it forthwith.

"More yet," the pilot went on, after a time. "She says there's another one, just as bad or worse. On your head, she says—no, on your head-bone—what the hell! Skull? No, *inside* your skull, she says now. Hell's bells, *I* don't know what she wants!"

"Maybe I do—keep still a minute." A telepath, undoubtedly, like the Manarkans—that was why she had to talk to her first. He'd never been around telepaths much—never tried it. He walked a few steps and stared directly into one pair of Luda's eyes. Large, expressive eyes, soft now, and gentle.

"That's it, Chief! Now blast easy—baffle your jets. Relax, she means. Open your locks and let her in!"

Cloud did relax, but gingerly. He did not like this mind-to-mind stuff at all, particularly when the other mind belonged to such a monster. He lowered his mental barriers skittishly, ready to revolt at any instant. But as soon as he began to understand the meaning of her thoughts he forgot utterly that he was not talking man to man. The interchange was not as specific nor as facile as is here to be indicated, of course, but every detail was eventually made perfectly clear.

"I demand Darjeeb's life!" was her first intelligible thought. "Not because he is my enemy and the enemy of all my race—that would not weigh with you—but because he has done what no one else, however base, has ever been so lost to shame as to do. In the very capital of our city upon Lune he kindled an atomic flame which is killing us in multitudes. In case you do not know about atomic flames, they can never be—"

"I know—we call them loose atomic vortices. But they can be extinguished. That is my business, putting them out."

"Oh—incredible but glorious news!" Luda's thoughts seethed, became incomprehensible. Then, after a space, "To win your help for my race I perceive that I must be completely frank with you," she went on. "Observe my mind closely, please, so that you may see for yourself that I am withholding nothing. Darjeeb wants at any cost the secret of your vessels' speed. With it his race will destroy mine utterly. I want it too, of course—if I could obtain it we would wipe out the Uhalians. However, since you are so much more powerful than could be believed possible, I realize that I am helpless. I tell you, therefore, that both Darjeeb and I have long since summoned help. Warships of both sides are approaching to capture one or both of these vessels. Darjeeb's are nearest, and these secrets must not, under any conditions, go to Uhal. Dash out into space with both of these vessels, so that we can plan at leisure. First, however, kill that unspeakable murderer. You have scarcely injured him the way it is. Or, free me, give me that so-deceptive little axe, and I will be only too glad—"

A chain snapped ringingly, and metal clanged against metal. Only two of Darjeeb's major arms had been incapacitated; his two others had lost only a few fingers apiece from their respective hands. His immense bodily strength was almost unimpaired; his feeding hand was untouched. He could have broken free at any time, but he had waited, hoping that he could take Cloud by surprise or that some opportunity would arise for him to regain control of this lifeboat. But now, deeming it certain that the armored biped would follow Luda's eminently sensible advice, he decided to let inertialessness go for the time being, in the interest of saving his own life.

"Kill him!"

Luda shrieked the thought and Cloud swung his weapon aloft. But Darjeeb was not attacking. Instead, he was rushing into the airlock—escaping!

"Go free, pilot!" Cloud commanded, and leaped; but the heavy valve swung shut before he could reach it.

As soon as the lock could be operated the Tellurian went through it. He knew that Darjeeb could not have boarded the cruiser, since every port was locked. He hurried to his control room and scanned space. There the Uhalian was, falling like a plummet under the combined forces of his own drive and the gravitations of two worlds. There also were a dozen or so spaceships, too close for comfort, blasting upward.

Cloud cut in his Bergenholm, kicked on his driving blasts, cut off, and went back into the lifeboat.

"Safe enough now," he announced. "They'll never get out here inert. I'm surprised that he jumped—didn't think he was the type to kill himself."

"He isn't. He didn't," Luda said, dryly.

"Huh? He must have! That was a mighty long flit he took and his suit wouldn't hold air."

"He would stuff something into the holes—if necessary he could make it the whole distance without either air or armor. He is tough. He still lives—curse him! But it is of no use for me to bewail that fact now. Let us make plans. You must extinguish that flame and the leaders of our people will have to convince you that—"

"Just a sec—quite a few things we've got to do first." He fell silent.

First of all, he had to report to the Patrol, so that they could get Lensmen and a battle fleet out here to straighten up this mess. With his short-range communicators, that would take some doing—but wait, he had a double-ended tight beam to the Laboratory. He could get through on that, probably, even from here. He'd have to mark the lifeboat as a derelict and get these folks aboard his cruiser. No space-tube. He had an extra suit, so he could transfer the women easily enough, but this Luda....

"Don't worry about me!" that entity cut in, sharply. "You saw how I came aboard here, didn't you? I do not particularly enjoy breathing a vacuum, but I can stand it—I am as tough as Darjeeb is. So hurry, please hurry. During every moment we delay, more of my people are dying!"

CHAPTER FOUR

Two Worlds for Conquest!

When Luda had given him the entire picture, Cloud saw that it was far from bright. Darjeeb's coup had been planned with surpassing care and been executed brilliantly; his spies and fifth columnists had known exactly what to do and had done it in perfect synchronization with the armed forces striking from without. Drugged, betrayed by her own officers, Luda had been carried off without a struggle. She did not know just how far-reaching the stroke had been, but she feared that most of the fortresses were now held by the enemy.

Uhal probably had the advantage in numbers and in power of soldiers and warships then upon Lune—Darjeeb would not have made his bid unless he had been able in some way to get around the treaty of strict equality in armament. Dhil was, however, much the nearer of the two worlds. Therefore, if this initial advantage could be overcome, Dhil's main forces could be brought into action much sooner than could the enemy's. And if, in addition, the vortex could be extinguished before it had done too much irreparable damage, neither side would have any real tactical advantage and the conflict would subside instead of flaring up into another world-girdling holocaust.

Cloud would have to do something, but what? That vortex had to be snuffed out—but defended as it was by Uhalians in the air and upon the ground, how could he make the approach?

His vortex-bombing flitter was screened only against the frequencies of atomic disintegration; she could not ward off for a minute the beams of even the feeblest ship of war. His cruiser was clothed to stop anything short of a mauler's primary blasts, but there was no possible way of using her as a vehicle from which to bomb the vortex out of existence. He had to analyze the thing first, preferably from a fixed ground-station. Then, too, his special instruments were all in the flitter, and the cruiser had no bomb-tubes.

How could he use what he had to clear a station? The cruiser had no offensive beams, no ordinary bombs, no negabombs.

"Draw me a map, will you please, Luda?" he asked.

She did so. The cratered vortex, where an immense building had once been; the ring of fortresses, two of which were unusually far apart, separated by a parkway and a shallow lagoon.

"Shallow? How deep?" Cloud interrupted. She indicated a depth of a couple of feet.

"That's enough map then—thanks." The physicist ruminated. "You seem to be quite an engineer. Can you give me details on your power plants, screen generators, and so on?" She could. Complex mathematical equations flashed through his mind, each leaving a residue of fact.

"Can be done, maybe—depends." He turned to the Chickladorian.

"Are you a pilot, or just an emergency assignment?"

"Pilot—master pilot. Rating unlimited, tonnage or space."

"Good! Think you're in shape to take three thousand centimeters of acceleration?"

"Pretty sure of it. If I was right I could take it standing on my head without a harness, and I'm feeling better all the time. Let's hot her up and find out."

"Not until after we've unloaded the passengers somewhere." Cloud went on, with the aid of Luda's map, to explain exactly what he had in mind.

"Afraid it can't be done." The pilot shook his head glumly. "Your timing has got to be too ungodly fine. I can do the piloting—determine power-to-mass ratio, measure the blast, and so on. I'm not afraid of balancing her down on her tail. I can hold her steady to a centimeter, but piloting's only half the job you want. Pilots don't ever land on a constant blast, and the leeway you allow here is damn near zero. To hit it as close as you want, your timing has got to be accurate pretty near to a tenth of a second. You don't know it, friend, but it'd take a master computer an hour to—"

"I know all about that. I'm a master computer and I'll have everything figured. I'll give you your zero in plenty of time."

"QX, then—what are we waiting for?"

"To unload the passengers. Luda, do you know of a place where they will be safe? And maybe you had better send a message to Dhil, to call out your army and navy. We can't blow out that vortex until we control the city, both in the air and on the ground."

"That message was sent long since. They are even now in space. We will land your women there." She pointed to a spot upon the plate.

They landed, but three of the women would not leave the vessel. The Manarkan declared that she had to stay aboard to take care of the patient. What would happen if he passed out again, with nobody except laymen around? She was right, Cloud conceded. And she could take it. She was a Manarkan, built of whalebone and rubber. She would bend under 3+ G's, but she wouldn't break.

The squatty insisted upon staying. Since when had a woman of Tominga hidden from danger or run away from a good fight? She could help the pilot hold his head up through an acceleration that would put Cloud into a pack—or give her that dureum axe and she'd show him how it *ought* to be swung!

The Chickladorian girl, too, remained aboard. Her eyes—not pink, but a deep, cool green, brimming with unshed tears—flashed at the idea of leaving her man to die alone. She just knew that they were all going to die. Even if she couldn't be of any use, even if she did have to be in a hammock, what of it? If her Thlaskin died she was going to die too, and that was all there was to it. If they made her go ashore she'd cut her own throat right then, so there!

And that was that.

A dozen armed Dhilians came aboard, as pre-arranged, and the cruiser blasted off. Then, while Thlaskin was maneuvering inert, to familiarize himself with the controls and to calibrate the blast, Cloud brought out the four semi-portable projectors. They were frightful weapons, so heavy that it took a strong man to lift one upon Earth. So heavy that they were designed to be mounted upon a massive tripod while in use. They carried no batteries or accumulators, but were powered by tight beams from the mother ship.

Luda was right; such weapons were unknown in that solar system. They had no beam transmission of power. The Dhilian warriors radiated glee as they studied the things. They had more powerful stuff, of course, but it was all fixed-mount, wired solid and far too heavy to move. This was wonderful—these were magnificent weapons indeed!

High above the stratosphere, inert, the pilot found his exact location and flipped the cruiser around, so that her stern pointed directly toward his objective upon the planet beneath. Then, using his forward, braking jets as drivers, he blasted her straight downward. She struck atmosphere almost with a thud. Only her fiercely-driven meteorite-screens and wall-shields kept her intact.

"I hope you know what you're doing, chum," the pilot remarked conversationally as the scene enlarged upon his plate with appalling rapidity. "I've made hot landings before, but I always figured on having a hair or two of leeway. If you don't hit this to a hundredth we're going to splash when we strike—we won't bounce!"

"I can compute zero time to a thousandth and I can set the clicker to within a hundredth, but it's you that'll have to do the real hitting." Cloud grinned back at the iron-nerved pilot. "Sure a four-second call is enough for you to get your rhythm, allow for reaction-time and lag, and blast exactly on the click?"

"Absolutely. If I can't get it in four I can't get it at all. Pretty close now, ain't it?"

"Uh-huh." Cloud, staring at the electro-magnetic reflection-altimeter which indicated continuously their exact distance above objective, began to sway his shoulders. He was more than a master computer. He knew, without being able to explain how he knew, every mathematical fact and factor of the problem. Its solution was complete. He knew the exact point in space and the exact instant in time at which the calculated deceleration must begin; by the aid of the sweep second-hand of the chronometer—one full revolution of the dial every second—he was now setting the clicking mechanism so that it would announce that instant. His hand swayed back and forth—a finger snapped down—and the sharp-toned instrument began to give out its crisp, precisely-spaced clicks.

"Got it on the hair!" Cloud snapped. "Get ready, Thlaskin. Seconds! Four! Three! Two! One! Click!"

Exactly upon the click the cruiser's driving blasts smashed on. There was a cruelly wrenching shock as everything aboard acquired suddenly a more-than-three-times-Earthly weight.

The Dhilians merely twitched. The Tomigan, standing behind the pilot's seat, supporting and steadying his wounded head in its rest, settled almost imperceptibly, but her firmly gentle hands did not yield a millimeter. The nurse sank deeply into the cushioned bench upon which she was lying, her quick, bright eyes remaining fixed upon her patient. The Chickladorian girl, in her hammock, fainted quietly.

And downward the big ship hurtled, tail first, directly toward the now glowing screens of a fortress. Driving jets are not orthodox weapons. But properly applied, they can become efficient ones indeed, and these were being applied with micrometric exactitude.

Down—down—down! The frantic Uhalians thought that it was crashing—thought it a suicide ship. Nevertheless, they fought it. The threatened fortress and its neighbors hurled out their every beam; the Uhalian ships dived frantically at the invader and tried their best to blast her down.

In vain. The cruiser's screens carried the load effortlessly.

Down she drove. The fortress' screens flamed ever brighter, radiating ever higher under the terrific bombardment. Closer—hotter! Nor did the frightful blast waver appreciably; the Chickladorian was a master pilot. Down!

"Set up a plus ten, Thlaskin," Cloud ordered quietly. "I missed it a bit—air density and the beams. Give it to her on the third click from ... *this*!"

"Plus ten it is, sir—on!"

A bare hundred yards now, and the ship of space was still plunging earthward at terrific speed. The screens were furiously incandescent, but were still holding.

A hundred feet. Velocity appallingly high, the enemy's screens still up. Something would *have* to give now. If that screen stood up, the ship must surely strike it, and vanish as she did so. But Thlaskin the Chickladorian made no move nor spoke no word to hike his blast. If the skipper was willing to bet his own life on his computations, who was he to squawk? But ... was it possible that Cloud had miscalculated?

No! While the mighty vessel's driving projectors were still a few yards away the defending screens exploded into blackness. The full awful streams of energy raved directly into the structures beneath. Metal and stone glared white, then flowed—sluggishly at first, but ever faster and more mobile—then boiled coruscantly into vapor.

The cruiser slowed—stopped—seemed to hang poised. Then slowly, reluctantly, she moved upward, her dreadful exhausts continuing the devastation.

"That's computin', mister," the pilot breathed. "To figure a dive like that right on the nose an' then to have the guts to hold her cold—skipper, that's computation!"

"All yours, pilot," Cloud demurred. "All I did was give you the dope—you're the guy that made it good."

High in the stratosphere the Chickladorian cut the acceleration to a thousand and Cloud took stock.

"Hurt, anybody?" Nobody was. "QX. We'll repeat, then, on the other side of the lagoon."

And as the cruiser began to descend upon the new course the vengeful Dhilian fleet arrived upon the scene. Looping, diving, beaming, often crashing in suicidal collision, the two factions went maniacally to war. Friend and foe alike, however, avoided the plunging Tellurian ship. That monster, they had learned, was a thing about which they could do nothing.

The second fortress fell exactly as the first had fallen, and as the pilot brought the cruiser gently to ground in the middle of the shallow lake, Cloud saw that the Dhilians, overwhelmingly superior in numbers now, had cleared the air of the ships of Uhal.

"Can you fellows and your ships keep them off of my flitter while I take my readings?" he demanded.

"We can," the natives radiated, happily. Four of the armored bone-heads were *wearing* the semi-portables. They had them perched lightly atop their feeding heads, held immovably in place by two huge arms apiece. One hand sufficed to operate the controls, leaving two hands free to whatever else might prove in order.

"Let us out!"

The lock opened, the Dhilian warriors sprang out and splashed away to meet the foot-soldiers who were already advancing into the lagoon.

Cloud watched pure carnage for a few minutes. He hoped—yes, there they were! The loyalists, seeing that their cause was not lost after all, had hastily armed themselves and were coming into the fray. There would be no tanks—the navy would see to that.

The Blaster broke out his flitter then, set it down near the vortex, and made his observations. Everything was normal. The sigma curve was the spectacularly unpredictable thing which he had come to expect. He selected three bombs from the cruiser's vast store, loaded them into the tubes, and lofted. He set his screens, adjusted his goggles, and waited, while far above him and wide around him his guardian Dhilian war-vessels toured watchfully, their drumming blasts a reassuring thunder.

He waited, eyeing the sigma curve as it flowed backward from the tracing pen, until finally he could get a satisfactory ten-second prediction. That is, he knew that ten seconds thence, the activity of the vortex would match, closely enough, one of his bombs. He shot his flitter forward, solving instantaneously the problems of velocity and trajectory. At exactly the correct instant he released the bomb. He swung his little bomber aside, went inertialess....

The bomb sped truly. Into that awful crater, through that fantastic hell of heat and of lethal radiation and of noxious gas. It struck the vortex itself, dead center. It penetrated just deeply enough. The extremely refractory casing of neocarballoy, so carefully computed as to thickness, held just long enough. The carefully-weighed charge of duodec exploded, its energy and that of the vortex combining in a detonation whose like no inhabitant of that solar system had even dimly imagined.

The gases and the pall of smoke and pulverized tufa blew aside; the frightful waves of fluid lava quieted down. The vortex was out and would remain out. The Vortex Blaster went back to his cruiser and stored his flitter away.

"Oh, you did it—thanks! I didn't believe, really, that you—that anybody—could do it!" Luda was almost hysterical in her joyous relief.

"Nothing to it," Cloud deprecated. "How are your folks coming along with the mopping up?"

"Practically clean," Luda answered, grimly. "We now know who is who, I think. Those who fought against us or who did not fight for us very soon will be dead. But the Uhalian fleet comes. Does yours? Ours goes to meet it in moments."

"Wait a minute!" Cloud sat down at his plate, made observations and measurements, calculated mentally. He energized his longest-range communicator and conferred briefly.

"The Uhalian fleet will be here in seven hours and eighteen minutes. If your people go out to meet them it will mean a war that not even the Patrol can stop without destroying practically all of the ships and men you have in space. The Patrol flotilla will arrive in seven hours, thirty-one minutes. Therefore I suggest that you hold your fleet here, in formation but quiescent, under instructions not to move until you yourself signal them to do so, while you and I go out and see if we can't stop the Uhalians."

"*Stop* them?" Luda's thought was a distinctly unladylike one. "What with, pray?"

"I don't know," Cloud confessed, "but it wouldn't do any harm to try, would it?"

"No—probably not." And so it was done.

All the way out Cloud pondered ways and means. As the cruiser neared the on-rushing fleet he sent a quick thought to Luda:

"Darjeeb is undoubtedly with that fleet. He knows that this is the only inertialess ship in this part of space. He wants it worse than he wants anything else in the universe. Now, if we could only make him listen to reason—if we could make him see—"

He broke off. No soap. You couldn't explain "green" to the blind. These folks didn't know and wouldn't believe what real power was. Any one of those oncoming Patrol super-dreadnoughts could blast both of these combined fleets clear out of space. Those primary beams were starkly incredible to anyone who had never seen them in action. The Uhalians didn't stand the chance of a fly under a mallet, but they would have to be killed before they'd believe it. A damned shame, too. The joy, the satisfaction, the real advancement possible only through cooperation with each other and with the millions of races of Galactic Civilization—if there were only some means of *making* them believe—

"We—and they—*do* believe!" Luda broke in upon his somber musings.

"Huh? What? You do? You were listening?" Cloud exclaimed.

"Certainly. At your first thought I put myself en rapport with Darjeeb, and he and his people—all of us—listened to your thoughts."

"But—you *really* believe me?"

"We believe, all of us, but some will cooperate only as far as it seems to serve their own ends to do so. Your Lensmen, if they are able to, will undoubtedly have to kill that insect Darjeeb and—"

The insulted Uhalian drove in a protesting thought, but Luda went calmly on, "You think, then, Tellurian, that your Lensmen can cope with even such as Darjeeb of Uhal?"

"I'll say they can!"

"It is well, then. Come aboard, Darjeeb—unarmed and unarmored, as I am. We will together go to confer with these visiting Lensmen of Galactic Civilization. It is understood that there is to be no warfare until our return."

"Holy Klono!" Cloud gasped. "He wouldn't do *that*, would he?"

"Certainly." Luda was surprised at the question. "Although he is an insect, and is morally and ethically beneath contempt, he is, after all, a reasoning being."

"QX." Cloud was dumbfounded, but tried manfully not to show it. "In that case everything can be settled without another blow being struck."

Darjeeb came aboard the cruiser. He was heavily bandaged and most of his hands were useless, but he apparently bore no ill-will whatever. Cloud gave orders; the ship flashed away to meet the oncoming Patrolmen.

The conference was held, coming out precisely as Luda had foreseen. The fleets returned, each to its home world, and plenipotentiaries of Dhil and of Uhal held long meetings with the Lensmen.

"You won't need me any more, will you, Admiral?" Cloud asked, a few days later.

"No. Nice job, Cloud."

"Thanks. I think I'll be on my way, then—clear ether!" And the Vortex Blaster, after taking leave of his other new friends, resumed his interrupted voyage—having added another solar system to the fellowship of Galactic Civilization!

---

[1] For the explanation of these somewhat peculiar facts, which is too long to go into here, the reader is referred to *Transactions of the Planetographical Society; Vol. 283, No. 11, p. 2745.*—E.E.S.

www.ingramcontent.com/pod-product-compliance
Ingram Content Group UK Ltd.
Pitfield, Milton Keynes, MK11 3LW, UK
UKHW042152281224
453045UK00004B/357